SAM'S
First Birthday

written by Rebekah Stion
for Johnny

illustrated by Lorraine Arthur

Library of Congress Catalog Card No. 85-62953

© 1986. The STANDARD PUBLISHING Company, Cincinnati, Ohio
Division of STANDEX INTERNATIONAL Corporation. Printed in U.S.A.

"Sam, I'm glad we have this special place!" said Dean, as they crawled into their playhouse. There was just enough room for the two of them. The tin roof almost touched Dean's head. The straw floor was like a carpet. It was fun to have a picnic with Sam.

Sam's tail began to wag as Dean spread their picnic lunch. Dean thanked God for their food. He also thanked God for Sam. Eight months had passed since Sam had arrived at Dean's house. These had been the happiest months of Dean's life. He was so glad to have his special friend. Sam had been born on Christmas Day the year before. Now it was November already. Sam would soon be having his first birthday!

As Dean finished his last piece of chicken, he heard a horn blow. He knew his dad was calling him. Dean crawled out of the playhouse with Sam.

Dean whistled a happy tune as he ran with Sam across the yard.

Dean saw that his dad was working on his truck. He stopped to help him.

Suddenly there was a loud noise in front of the house. Sam barked one time.

Dean's mother rushed out of the house. "Something has happened to Sam!" she said.

Everyone rushed around the house. Sam was lying in the middle of the street. He had been hit by a car.

"Oh, no!" cried Dean.

Dean's father ran as fast as he could to Sam. He picked Sam up and carried him into the house.

"Sam is not breathing," said Dad.

Dean watched as his dad pushed hard into Sam's chest. Then he pushed again. Sam wasn't breathing. His dad looked very sad.

As Dean's mother knelt down beside them, Dean began to pray, "Thank You, God, for giving Sam to me. Please don't let him ... "

Dean's dad pushed once again on Sam's chest. A big smile came across his face.

"Sam is breathing!" he said happily. "We must take Sam to the animal hospital right away. He is going to need special care."

Dean and his mother rushed Sam to the hospital. The doctor who treated Sam was very kind and gentle.

"Sam has a broken back leg and bruises," said the doctor. "We will give him special care. You can take him home tomorrow."

Dean patted Sam good-bye. He knew that leaving Sam at the hospital overnight would be best. Dean thought about God's love. He was glad he could talk to God about everything. He prayed and thanked God that Sam was going to live.

The next morning Dean was excited about seeing Sam. He dressed in a hurry.

"I have good news for you, Dean," said his mother at breakfast. "The doctor called this morning. We can pick Sam up at two o'clock this afternoon. He is going to be fine. The doctor put Sam's broken leg in a cast. He will have to wear it for six weeks. After that Sam will be as good as new."

At two o'clock Dean and his mother walked into the animal hospital. They were eager to see Sam.

The doctor brought Sam to Dean. Sam licked Dean's hand. Dean thanked the doctor for taking good care of Sam.

Every day Sam grew stronger. He learned how to hold his leg and walk.

The six weeks passed. The day arrived when Sam's cast would be removed. Dean and his mother took Sam to the animal hospital.

The doctor cut the tape from the metal bars around Sam's leg.

Sam stood up and tried to walk. The leg didn't want to move.

"As Sam uses the leg, it will become stronger," said the doctor.

The good news made Dean happy as they drove home. He held Sam close and thought about God's love. He silently thanked God again for Sam's recovery.

Arriving at home, Dean's mother surprised him.

"Dean," she said, "would you like to help me put up the Christmas tree tonight?"

"Oh, yes, Mother!" said Dean. "I had almost forgotten Christmas is only two weeks away, and it's Sam's birthday, too."

After the evening meal they decorated the tree. Then Dean's dad reached for the family Bible. They gathered around the tree for a special devotion time. Dean listened as his dad read about Jesus the Savior being born.

"The birth of Jesus was God's way of saying, I love you," said Dean's dad.

Dean always loved Christmas when his family celebrated the birth of Jesus. They gave gifts to family, friends, and others. This was their way of showing God's love.

Dean grew excited as he marked off each day on the calendar. Five, four, three, two, one, and then Christmas Day arrived!

Christmas morning Dean's mother and dad heard noises. They knew Dean and Sam were at the Christmas tree.

Dean was putting a beautiful heart collar around Sam's neck. Dean's grandmother had put the gift for Sam under the tree on Christmas eve.

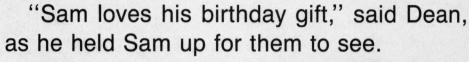

"Sam loves his birthday gift," said Dean, as he held Sam up for them to see.

"This is a special first birthday for Sam," said Dean. "He is alive and healthy."

As Dean sat near the Christmas tree, he remembered God's love. He understood the true meaning of Christmas. He had joy in his heart, and he was going to share it with everyone. That would be what God wanted him to do.